DARK CORNER

SHORT HORROR STORIES

VOL.1

DREW NICKS

MARY FRANCES CAVALLARO

ROBERT SABALA

DARK CORNER

SHORT HORROR STORIES

VOL.1

INDEX

THE OUTER WORLDS
DREW NICKS

The dreary October rain held downtown Boston in its miserable grasp. It was midday, but most would be hard pressed to tell it from any other point of day. The rain showers had not abated in nearly three weeks. In the slick streets, people scurried about. Rain splashed off hats and umbrellas alike.

Professor Roderick Tharpe despaired over the gloomy grayness that lay just outside the yellow cab's windowpane. He had never liked Boston; despised the roving moisture that was ever present. Now that he was here his hate had grown. Leaning forward, he queried the cabbie:

"How much further, cabbie? There is much I still need to do and I've such little time to do it. Do you understand me?"

The cabbie shot Tharpe a harsh and burning glare in the rear-view mirror.

"Listen buddy," said the cabbie. "I couldn't give a rat's ass who you are or what you need to do. Frankly, I don't know what an old geezer like you wants in sleaze central. This is Boston, man, as much as I try to use my mind to make people move, it don't work."

The cabbie went silent but not before shooting Tharpe the worst evil eye he could muster. His eyes then fell back to the road, content to focus his anger elsewhere.

Tharpe knew when the time was right to remain quiet, so he took this opportunity to remain silent. With his liver spotted hands he began to grope around the cab's floor. After a moment, he had it and sitting on his lap was a well aged, partially stained leather briefcase. With long skeletal fingers Tharpe thumbed the combination on the clasps. A resounding pop, and then before him lay his years of research.

Had it really been 25 years now?

As he fondly looked at photos and Xeroxes of days

gone by he began to think about all the time and effort. He had been on a great number of chases in this past quarter century. Sometimes it felt like he had been to the end of the world and back again. In a way he had; traversing uncharted mountainous regions in China and Tibet, hacking wildly through dense undergrowth in the least travelled sections of dark East Africa and even a rare, one time opportunity to visit the Antarctic. All of these labors had proven fruitless. The closest he had ever come to the truth was in the mountains of Hungary. After hearing many legends of a shunned village he'd finally ascertained its whereabouts. Upon entering Stregoicavar, he had had a difficult time locating a guide to take him to The Black Stone. He had chalked it up to superstition but, mentally, hoped that the legends had perhaps been true. When he finally did have a guide, the guide would go no further than a half mile from The Black Stone. Alone in the wooded glen that surrounded the stone, Tharpe had been certain he had seen something. He had felt so incredibly close, yet it was to no avail.

That had been 15 years ago; and while he still searched he had come no closer. However, the last 2 months had proven very fruitful to the Professor. While at a get to-gether for former staff, students and luminaries from Miskatonic University he had met a man who claimed he could help Roderick in his seemingly never-ending quest. He had said there was a very unique bookstore in Boston which may have what Tharpe looked for. The man said the place was called "Blake's Specialty and Oc-cult Books" and that he had heard, in good faith, that the place was a historical repository. Manuscripts from as far back as the Roman era were supposedly held in its care.

This, Tharpe knew, had to be the place that would fi-nally put an end to this journey. While staring out at the bleak, grey atmosphere that shrouded Boston he felt the cab's motion come to a halt. As he laid his eyes across the street, he saw the bright neon of "Blake's Specialty and Occult Books"

The shop sat sandwiched between an adult book-store and an Asian "massage" parlor. Its exterior plain-ly showed that it had not been repainted in sometime. Peeling green paint revealed itself through the dense fog. What really drew Tharpe's attention were the eso-teric, neon symbols shining brightly in the shops large bay window. These were symbols he immediately recognized. The Elder Sign. The Eye of Light and Darkness. The fabled Sign of Koth. He was lost in a trance. Everything in the waking world around him seemed insignificant and futile.

"Hey buddy, you gonna pay me or what?"

Tharpe snapped out of his daze long enough to absent-mindedly paw for his wallet. He paid the cabbie and soon found himself standing in the oppressive fog of the Boston afternoon.

Blake's Specialty and Occult Books was usually spoken of in the hushed tones of eccentric groups in and around Boston. For a city with such a long history the darkness had never been far behind. The Blake family had held some renown in Boston's upper class for several centuries. They were never held in high esteem, but they were an ever present part of high society. Roger Blake, the current proprietor, had been a fixture about Boston for at least the last 3 decades. People tried best to avoid the remaining Blake as the family's history had led many to shun the name. Nevertheless, the people who had spoken to Roger had only the most positive things to say about the slightly odd man.

The nearly derelict appearance of the exterior of the building led Tharpe to believe the money had long since disappeared. After studying the markings in the window a moment longer, he took a deep breath and casually strolled across the empty street. Standing before the door, he marveled at the intricate carvings on the old piece of Victorian wood. It almost took on the appearance of a Bosch painting. Everything seemed so life like. Finally he mustered the courage to enter the beaten building.

The small bell that hung above the doorway jingled to introduce Tharpe's entry. For what seemed almost an eternity Tharpe stood in awe. Not only was the interior better maintained than the exterior, the same carvings that covered the exterior door were repeated in the beautiful woodwork of the interior. The carvings made Tharpe think of Dante's *Inferno*, with their nearly biblical yet oddly alien appearance. This was not what truly drew his eye, though. For lining every available inch of wall space were piles upon piles of books. The smell of centuries old paper and leather brought a euphoric sensation to his brain. Not since he had been to Europe had he been so enraptured by this scent.

The bindings on the volumes began to reveal to him the true stories of some of these works. Some were better bound than others. Some were gilded in the most majestic metals. These, he thought, were likely from the renaissance period. While still others seemed very crudely bound in other strange materials. Volumes wrapped in animal hide seemed the most prevalent, but hidden amongst these were volumes bound in some of the strangest metals Tharpe could ever comprehend. Moving to a shelf, he withdrew a particularly odd looking hide bound tome. The spine did little to reveal the contents; it was only when he held it in his hands that he realized the true source of its binding. This volume appeared to be bound in human skin. The face that stared back at Tharpe sent chills down his spine. The gaping maw of a mouth must've spent several centuries as someone's nightmare.

As he looked more intently around the shop the titles started to draw him in. Here, before his very eyes, were many of the oldest editions of antique grimoires he had ever seen. Prinn's *De Vermiis Mysteriis.* Von Junzt's *Unaussprechlichen Kulten.* Even a manuscript copy of Justin

Geoffrey's *The People of the Monolith*. Tharpe's mind was agog with the possibilities that this shop may contain. With his roving eyes he even spotted an original Arabic copy of Alhazred's *Necronomicon.* The bright crimson lettering which read *Kitab Al-Aazif,* sent his mind racing a million directions at once. For the first time since he had come to Boston, he felt close to his final goal.

As he stood gawking at the vast collection he felt as though he was being watched. The hairs on the back of his neck stood on end. Slowly, he turned to face this perceived threat. For reasons unknown, even to himself, he turned with his eyes closed. When he opened them he saw, to his relief, that the threat he was expecting was not so. Before him stood a stocky, bald elderly man. The old man wore a slightly tattered Brown University sweater. Judging from its age Tharpe theorized it was likely from the 30's or 40's. The old man's face was riddled with the crevices and canyons of a well spent life. His grey eyes looked very tired but belied a strong sense of power and knowledge. But his most out-standing feature was the neatly trimmed goatee on the man's chin. If one were to squint the man almost looked liked an elderly Satan.

The Professor extended his hand to the legendary Blake.

"You must be Roger Blake. I must admit, your collection is truly impressive."

Blake silently took Tharpe's extended hand and returned the shake. The older man had an impressively strong handshake for a man who must be near 90.

"I am, and who might you be?"

He loosed his grip on Tharpe's hand. Tharpe recoiled with, what he hoped was, hidden pain but he responded:

"My name is Roderick Tharpe. Professor of Antiquities at Miskatonic University."

Blake grimaced openly at Tharpe's words before he turned back to his hiding spot. Tharpe now noticed the desk that had been concealed by stacks of books that nearly reached the ceiling. This, he thought, is where that elderly creature had been hiding. He was about to comment before Blake said:

"Tharpe, eh? I've heard of you. I've heard about what others have called your mad quests and I take it that's why I find you here in my quaint little shop."

Tharpe laughed at the thought that this man considered his shop "quaint". Most shocking of all to the Professor was how would this man know my name? Were my exploits that widely known? Or have my colleagues come to this very shop to prepare the owner for my presence?

"That's one reason I'm here," replied Tharpe calmly. "I also wanted to see the marvelous collection that holds so many in envy."

Blake smiled mischievously.

"Ah, so you've come to see the oldest and the rarest," said Blake. "You do have fine tastes Mr. Tharpe. Would you like to see what I'm working on right now?"

Tharpe, his curiosity piqued, walked over to the concealed desk. Looking in the mighty stacks, he saw rougher and even rarer tomes. Atop one stack sat a mold ridden copy of the cursed *Book of Eibon*. From its delicately inlaid cover Tharpe could see it was a very, very early Greek translation.

Blake motioned for Tharpe to lay his eyes upon the centuries old book that lay in the middle of his clutter strewn desk. Roderick's eyes lit up at the antiquity that sat in front of him.

The small, leather bound book looked innocuous at

first unless one knew the tell tale signs they were look-ing for. The silver inlaid pentagram on the cover and the singed pages told the books troubled history. Tharpe stood in shocked silence.

"*The Nine Gates of the Kingdom of Shadows,*" said Tharpe, as he stood in awe of its superb engravings. "By Aristide Torchia. That's the first copy I've ever seen in all my years."

Blake chuckled.

"Your reputation precedes you, Professor. Let us cut to the chase. I know you didn't just come to admire an old man's collection. What is it that you want?"

Tharpe was unsure how to introduce his proposition. Despite being around for 9 decades this man was still as sharp as a tack. There was certainly no fooling him. After several moments, he finally revealed his true in-tentions.

"You've seen through my veil," said Tharpe sheepish-ly. "I'm looking for a copy of *Et Determinatio Mundi, in Exterioribus Ultra.*"

Blake nearly fell from his chair. His breathing sud-denly became heavy and erratic. For a moment, Thar-pe feared, the old man would have a massive coronary.

Slowly, Blake steadied himself and his breathing calmed.

"*Channeling the Outer Worlds and Beyond,*" whispered Blake. "By Augustus Burrienus. I'm sorry to tell you Mr. Tharpe, but no copies exist of that hellish tome."

Now it was Roderick's turn to chuckle.

"Don't be so bashful. I know you own a copy. That's why my colleagues sent me here."

"Your colleagues were mistaken, Mr. Tharpe," said Blake vehemently. "Now please leave my store. I've much work to do and little time to do it."

Anger began to rise inside the mind of Roderick Tharpe. I've not come this far to be tossed aside like an inconvenience to some aged antiquarian.

"Don't play coy with me old man," sneered Tharpe as he stepped forward menacingly. "I know you've got it here; you just won't show it to me!"

Blake shot from his chair as quick as lightning. With comparable menace, he stood eye to eye with the Professor. The grey eyes that Tharpe looked into seemed to fluctuate like a storm clouds rolling in.

"Mr. Tharpe, that book is very powerful indeed. Those who cannot harness its power should not play idle games with it.

The old man stood so close to Tharpe that he could smell his acrid breath.

"Mr. Tharpe, if you don't leave immediately I shall be forced to call the police. So do us both a favor and leave."

Tharpe was barely able to halt the tremors of rage coursing through his body. But, with considerable effort, he turned himself round to face the Victorian front door. He took a final glance at the many volumes that lay scattered about the room. This insult cannot stand, he thought. When he turned to the old man he saw that he too was shaking with rage. This made Tharpe smile involuntarily.

"Mark my words, Blake, I'll be back and I will take I came for!"

He slammed the door with all the power he had, sending the bell careening to the floor. Its melodious tinkle ended in a dull thud.

That evening Tharpe began to form a plan. The old man is feeble, he thought, it should take no effort at all to overpower him. He mulled this thought over for many hours before he decided that this would be the only way. If the old man must die, he must die.

As the cab pulled away, Tharpe briefly had second thoughts. The dreary, moist atmosphere of Boston was acting harshly on his arthritis. I'm no longer the young man I once was. That thought hit him hard before he pushed it aside. I've not spent near an eternity searching to be outdone by my age and the threats of some feeble man! He readjusted his trench coat, fixing the collar so it nearly stood straight up and made his way towards Blake's Specialty and Occult books. The crowbar he carried in his briefcase weighed heavy on his left side…

Standing outside the shops darkened windows, Tharpe felt confident. The street was deserted at this hour. He looked to his watch. Nearly midnight. The perfect crime.

Ignoring the next door massage parlor, he crept to a small, wood framed window in an adjoining alley. Perched precariously on a stack of old pallets, Tharpe dug the crowbar into the brittle wood. The window itself nearly crumbled. He had to take quick action to catch the falling pane. Relieved, he placed the unbroken glass against the exterior wall of the parlor. Excitedly, he coerced his aching joints into climbing the 3 feet to the window. Like a badly out of practice snake, he wriggled through the darkened opening.

Tharpe hit the floor with a loud thump. He felt something snap in his back. The darkened interior of the store did not seem as inviting as it had before. As he stood, he winced with the pain. Probably a slipped disk, he thought, another grievance to report to the doctor. But, if this miraculous bookstore did contain the book he sought, he would never have to see the doctor again.

Lighting a flashlight, he surveyed his surroundings. The stacks of books loomed menacingly, like specters, about him. He scanned the spines and, as he'd suspected, the book he sought was not in sight. Scanning further, he saw a short hallway nearly hidden at the back of the store. He had some reservations about this hallway, for he could see a dim light. Tharpe had not been expecting this. The light must clearly have been emanating from a study which must be hidden in the back. Did the old man not have a home to go to? Did he know I was going to come? No matter, if there is a place where that man would be keeping this book, it must be in his private study. The insufferable swine!

Cautiously, Tharpe made his way down the hall trying his utmost to make his approach unheard. Despite the care he put into it, the floorboards argued with his stealth. Every single, board creaked loudly, as if the building itself was trying to reveal his approach. He cursed under his breath, thinking that maybe he should have taken his shoes off.

As quietly as he could he reached the open doorway. Cautiously peeking in, Tharpe saw the old man asleep at his desk. At least he appeared to be asleep. The horrible noises emanating from Blake Tharpe took for snoring. Like a cat, Tharpe crept quietly into the room. He looked about at Blake's private collection. Some of the titles kept in this small back room he could not even comprehend. The tall stacks of books directly on Blake's desk held some of the oddest hieroglyphs and pictograms Tharpe had ever seen. There was much this old man was not telling me, he thought.

As Tharpe moved closer to Blake he knew for certain the man was sleeping. His eyes seemed nearly pasted shut. His oddly patterned wheezes came at random intervals. Tharpes eyes drifted to the book that lay open on Blake's desk. There it lay. Though he could not see the cover, Tharpe knew from the engravings that this was *Et Determinatio Mundi, in Exteriorbus Ultra*. He cautiously moved his hands towards his final goal. As quietly as he could he closed its ancient, worm eaten pages. The feeling that welled inside Roderick Tharpe was near hysteria. He finally had it. *Now to make good on my escape…*

Tharpe turned to leave, cradling the book like a newborn infant. As he turned he felt a strong grasp on his right forearm. A voice calmly said to him:

"You're going to want to put that back. You don't want to face *his* wrath."

Before he even had time to think, Tharpe turned and smashed the crowbar down on the old man's head. Looking at the blood cascading down the face of the former Roger Blake, Tharpe suddenly realized that the old man had not moved at all. He still sat facing the wall. *It couldn't have been him who grabbed me; but if not him then who?* He pondered this for a moment.

Perhaps I'm losing it? This thought was soon replaced by the realization of the true gravity of the situation he was now in. *I just broke into a book store. I stole a very valuable book and, on top of that, I've just murdered the owner. I've got to get out of here.*

He turned and made a break for the door, knocking down a fair sized stack of books in the process. They collapsed to the floor, many disintegrated on impact. Tharpe didn't care. He had to leave. Now!

Standing at the front door he took one last second to marvel at the fantastical Bosch style carvings on old wooden door. Strange, he thought, they seem to have changed. No matter now. With the adrenaline still coursing through him, he threw open the big door and dashed across the threshold....

...only to find himself back in Blake's office. He looked about in confusion. How did this happen? How is this even possible? I'm certain that I went through the front door.

He made his way to Blake's office door once again, and then he noticed something peculiar. He turned and looked at Blake's office chair. The old man was not there. The blood stain still marked the old wooden floor where he had been slain but somehow he was gone. Not wanting to find out the answers to his questions, Tharpe once again made for the front door. Passing the disintegrated pile of books, he stopped dumbfounded. The front door was missing. He looked about in panic until he spotted the door, now located on the east wall. Wasn't there a bookshelf there, Tharpe questioned. The fear and panic overcame the questions as he crossed the room and ran through the door…

…. into Blake's office. Tharpe felt fear now. This can't be happening! The office seemed different now. Everything around him was now coated in a heavy layer of cobwebs. Large spiders scuttled across the dust en-crusted floor. Terror overwhelmed his mind as he wildly tried to find an exit. When he found himself out in the main library he gasped. All the books were gone, the bookshelves too. He looked down to the book he still had cradled in his arms. It evaporated to dust right be-fore his very eyes. Tharpe unleashed a shrill screech at the madness that was enveloping his mind.

An exit! Any exit! Tharpe thrashed wildly about the dusty shop. The front door had disappeared completely and even the window through which he had so illicitly entered was nowhere to be found.

"Get me out of here!"

Abruptly, the room grew colder. Tharpe began to shiver at the sudden change. All around him, he could feel some unseen presence lingering in the air. An unknown voice called to Tharpe:

"You requested the outer worlds," said the deep and sarcastic voice.

Tharpe felt the floor shudder beneath his feet. He looked down and then over to the walls. To his horror, the walls had begun to move inward. In blind panic, Tharpe hurled himself at the wall ahead of him. He hoped the drywall would be weak and collapse. The voice called again:

"Now you've got them!"

A look of realization crossed Tharpe's face. That voice, I've heard it before.

"Blake! That's you! I know it's you! Show yourself!"

The voice laughed. A deep, throaty, hellish laugh as Tharpe frantically tried to break through the wall as his surroundings drew nearer.

The remains of Professor Roderick Tharpe were discovered 9 days ago hidden in a dingy alley in east Boston. The body, if one could call it that, was so viciously mutilated it took dental records to identify the remains. Friends and colleagues reported that he had stated that he was going to Boston to visit a bookshop called "Blake's Specialty and Occult Books". A business license has not been issued for "Blake's Specialty and Occult Books" since 1964, incidentally the same year its proprietor died, one Roger Blake. The investigation is still ongoing....

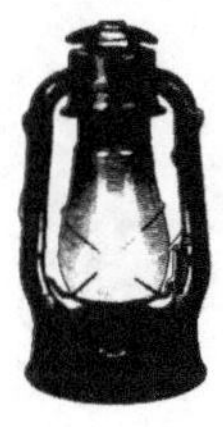

CELLAR DOOR

— MARY FRANCES CAVALLARO —

I expected a house with broken shutters, crumbling bricks, a pair of soulless eyes that peered out from the window on the second floor, and trees filled with crows that cawed "Death!"

In complete honesty, I imagined a house from one of those Gothic stories that I had read so often, a haunt of a place akin to the *House of Usher*, the front resembling a face, and the owners – brother and sister with a very *strange* relationship.

But this house was different. It was a blushing shade of pink with immaculate, snow-white shutters and a wraparound porch with intricate markings carved into the wood lining the ceiling. The only thing that struck me as odd – quite literally, as it jutted out from the side

33

of the house – was the faded wooden cellar door, shut tight with a rusty old lock; it wasn't even painted the same pink as the rest of the house, as if it weren't a part of the whole.

I pulled up to the front of the house in my carriage around midday, the coachman opening the door and tipping his hat, as is custom, to signal our arrival. I stepped down from the carriage, taking in the eerie calm; though the sun hadn't even begun to set, I felt something in the air that let me believe that at this place, at this little unsuspecting pink house, it was constantly night.

I steadied my resolve, walked up the stairs leading to the front door and knocked twice. A pretty young woman answered; she had long, flowing chestnut brown hair, a glowing complexion, and a smile that would make even the bleakest feel warmth inside their heart.

She inquired as to the purpose of my knocking and I replied, "I am here to help, Madam. It is my understanding that there is a need for a physician? I'm Dr. Branwyn."

She let me in and offered me a cup of tea. "That would be wonderful, thank you," I replied.

"Please, have a seat while you wait. Would you like cream and sugar?" she asked, pausing before heading to the kitchen.

"Thank you very much. And yes, I'll take both, please."

I removed my hat and sat down on a chair as I waited for the tea, taking it upon myself to look around the living room. The room was swathed in floral print, with chintz chairs to match, a cherry wood settee sofa covered in the very same pink that was all over the house. A simple sampler with the words "God Bless Our Home" cross-stitched into the linen was hung over the front door. The bookshelf held an impressive collection of novels, including *Fordyce's Sermons* and a King James Bible. All in all it seemed a cheery and cozy home.

I continued to inspect the room and landed my gaze upon the fireplace, ordinary in every respect expect for one item, preening front and center on the mantel. It was a bird figurine that could have fit in the palm of my hand, all blue-black feathers and beady peering eyes, that upon further inspection I surmised to be a raven. I assumed it to be nothing more than a family heirloom of sorts; why else would she permit such a macabre oddity to clash so harshly with the rest of her feminine domestications? I couldn't shake the feeling that something wasn't quite right. Amongst all the pink furniture and floral décor, all I could think of was that rusty lock upon the cellar door.

The young woman walked back into the living room carrying a tray of tea and cookies. She placed it down on the table and began to talk openly about herself, quite forgetting the reason that I was there. She spoke of her hobbies, her childhood memories, and most especially her family, a topic of particular interest to which she always rounded back in the conversation. I was patient and let her talk; it seemed she really had no one to talk to, and I didn't particularly mind lending an ear.

When she took a break in her stories, I intervened and reminded her why I was there. "Madam, I received a letter saying that someone was sick and needed help. Is the patient alright?" I asked, in the event of the illness being dire.

"Oh, of course… well never mind that right now. Now, where was I?" she shrugged it off and continued to talk, barely leaving room for me to intervene again in the hopes that I would forget why I was there. There was a patient in need of help and I was worried that I wouldn't be able to come to their aid in time.

The longer she talked, the darker my reflection became in the window panes as the sun shrunk from the moon's demanding glare; finally the surroundings were doing justice to the dark feeling in the air. I had not been able to shake that feeling of dread that I had felt from the moment I first arrived, and my heart beat faster and faster the longer that I stayed in the house.

This unsettling feeling in my body continued as my palms grew clammy and my chest constricted, as though my rapidly beating heart were caged behind ribs held tight with a rusty lock of a sternum.

The more my anxiety grew under the watchful eyes of the raven, the less patient I became, until I could no longer keep from asking her about its origin. I took a deep breath and said, "Madam, I beg your pardon, but I must ask you to indulge my rather abrupt curiosity. I have been intrigued by that raven figurine ever since I stole a moment's rest here on this chair. It stands out so starkly from the rest of the house that I couldn't help wonder from where it came," I said as I wiped a bead of sweat off my brow.

She paused, and a silence filled the room that lasted longer than any had since my visit to this strange little pink house had begun. She looked at me with hesitation and then looked up at the raven figurine perched on the fireplace, gripping the wood with its twisted claws as if ready to take flight 'round the room in a moment's notice.

"I could never get rid of it," she finally began, pronouncing the words slowly and carefully, as though each were sharp blades intending to keep her secrets hidden with a knick of the tongue.

"Would you mind giving further explanation? Where did you get it? It doesn't seem to be to your taste, in accordance with the rest of your home," I inquired.

She wasn't eager to answer; I could read it in her eyes as they shifted back and forth between the figurine and my own stock-still figure.

Choking on her words she replied, "The raven was given to me by my parents when I was a little girl."

"And how is your relationship with your parents?" I asked, trying to surmise the cause of her strong reaction.

"My relationship with my parents was the same as any other daughter's, I suppose. I did chores, took care of the house, prepared to be a good housewife." The unsteadiness in her voice and rattling of her spoon against her teacup as she tried to hold it steady in her hands convinced me that something was wrong.

"Madam, you can be honest, I won't judge you," I said, reassuring her that she could confide in me without it ever getting out.

No doubt she was nervous, but soon her words started flowing. "I love my parents very much. I want to make that clear. But my mother would constantly compare me to other girls in town…she said that I would never amount to anything. I tried. I tried so hard to be a daughter that they would unconditionally love and a woman they could be proud of, but no matter what I did, I was wrong. I had too many thoughts, too many opinions, spoke one too many words. She brought a Governess into our home to improve upon my etiquette, always got me invited to tea with only those neighbors of the best society. They required the Governess, a mean-spirited old woman, to take a birch switch to me, or lock me in a dark closet for hours until I repented. I would talk back and act out of turn, though I did try to behave for my parents. I could never make them proud, regardless of my actions. But I deserved it; I was such a bad girl. Such a bad girl." Her voice increased in volume and her speech became rapid the more she spoke.

"Madam! Madam!" I cried. "Calm down, it's alright." I paused for a minute and then spoke carefully, "why don't you try talking to them now?"

Tightening her grip on her teacup as she lowered it from her lips she answered, "I fear it's too late now... they're dead." Her eyes drowned in their tears despite how hard she tried to contain her emotions. She took a breath and continued on with the horrible tale. "The worst of it is, before they left on the night of the accident, we had gotten into an argument. They presented me with that very raven figurine, and I was thrilled to receive a gift from them, thinking it was a gesture of love, but they only uttered hurtful words. Mother looked at me with sheer contempt and said that I would appreciate such an object above a tea set or a new dress because it was just as bizarre and unseemly as myself. At that moment, I told them that they didn't appreciate anything I did or who I was and that I didn't love them, and would leave the confinement of their home as soon as I was able. Father made it easy to do that then, as he disinherited me with a few terse words."

"Oh Madam, I am sorry for your troubles. But you said that there was a much more horrid ending than the one you've provided thus far. What became of your parents that night?" I asked, both enthralled and horrified by her story.

"As I said, on that very night there was a dreadful accident. They were coming back from town in their carriage when something frightened the horses. The coachmen couldn't control the beasts and they were driven off the main road into a dense, desolate area of the forest. One of the wheels had cracked, and my parents sent the coachmen back into town to see if he could have it repaired. When he returned with the fixed wheel, he came upon a scene of carnage. As he described it to me during the investigation, he ran back into town and banged furiously upon the detective's door, waking him and everyone else close enough to hear with his loud, desperate cries of "Murder! Murder!"

The detective came to the house in the middle of the night...I had been awake, pacing the floors, crying, afraid of what would happen to me now that I wasn't welcome in my home. He knocked and gravely told me that my parents had been savagely murdered by a gang of thieves out for their belongings. I fainted from the shock, and came 'round to a doctor holding smelling salts under my nose. After that I don't remember much…it was all such a blur." She related the long, terrible tale and then stopped speaking to pour herself another cup of tea.

"My apologies, Madam. I had no idea," I said as she tried calming herself.

She collected herself quickly and said, "Oh, everything is completely fine now," wearing the very same cheerful smile on her face that she had greeted me with at the door.

I had been so engrossed in her story that I hadn't once checked the time, but the grandfather clock in the corner began to chime out reminders of the late hour, eleven in all. *Gong! Gong! Gong!* My heart sunk with each one.

"Oh my! I hadn't realized the time! Would you mind staying the night?" she asked. "It's much too dark for you to safely travel the roads." She quickly added, "You can get back to business in the morning…"

I was sure, just as with her stories, that this was merely another plot to get me to delay my work. I shuddered at the thought of having to stay even one night in this house that appeared so pleasant, but held such chill. However, I couldn't argue with her —it was late and I didn't want to be caught on these roads in the dark, especially after the story about her parents. How foolish of me, as I think back now, to fear the night more than the darkness that dwelled within the house. With no other choice, I swallowed past the lump in my throat and accepted her invitation.

She led me up the stairs to my room for the night by way of a dim oil lamp that lit up the pictures of guardian angels hanging on the walls. *How could I have thought this house was so bad?* I thought to myself as I walked up the stairs. The lady of the house bid me goodnight at the door to my bedchamber, and I settled in. I tossed and turned for the better of an hour (that felt like eternity). I simply couldn't sleep, though the bed felt just as the rest of the house appeared: quaint, comfortable, and completely unsuspecting.

I decided to throw off my tangled sheets and walk down to the kitchen for a cup of tea, hoping that it would calm my nerves. Walking down the corridor, it seemed much longer than it did when I had walked up, and the pictures of the guardian angels that once were calming now looked demonic. The holy figures had impish sneers, long snakelike tails, and twisted horns protruding from their foreheads. I noticed from the top step that the sign above the front door that one had written "God Bless Our Home" now read "Abandon All Hope Ye Who Enter Here." But I was just tired. My mind was merely playing tricks on me. *Wasn't it?*

I got downstairs and walked towards the kitchen, but stopped short when I felt a chilling sensation as I passed a dull pink door, nearly hidden in the wall save for the brass doorknob sticking out from its side, imploring me to enter. I reached for the doorknob but when I tried to open the door, the chain on the other side kept me from getting through. I fiddled around with the chain and, eventually, the lock came undone.

When I opened the door a gust of cold air blew in my face and gave me goose bumps, making the hairs on the back of my neck stand up. *It's just a draft*, I thought, pulling my jacket tighter around my chest. I noticed the rickety wooden staircase leading down into the basement and realized that this could only be the inside entrance to the cellar.

The further I descended, the more that I felt that dreary feeling that I had had all along, that dark chill that made my heart burst out of my chest, my muscles tense, and my body break out into a cold sweat. I gasped when I felt something brush against my forehead, and reached up to grab the offending horror-that-awaited.

I jumped back when I heard the scurry of a mouse pass and dropped the lamp that I'd had clutched in my hand. It broke and caught fire, making the darkness skitter into the corners along with my senseless fears… senseless until I looked up.

The lifeless body swung back-and-forth above my head, with two coffins lying only a few feet away, long-dead rotted corpses inside their dark confines. The Madam was dead! A note and a chair kicked on its side lay under her dangling feet.

I took the wooden stairs two at a time, ignoring their groans under the weight of my feet and ran out the front door, straight past the intricate carvings on the front porch and down to my carriage. I shook my coachman awake and urged him forward into the night, ignoring his baffled protests and inquiries. We headed back to the asylum immediately, my mind replaying the scene over and over in my head without any comprehension. I was new to the institution; I had never seen a patient dead. I knew nothing of this Madam, except that she had been released from the asylum for good behavior. It was supposed to be a routine check-up on a "cured" patient. *It wasn't supposed to be this way.*

A few days later a story in the paper read, "The uncontrollable fire devoured the entire house; the pink curtains and furniture, the bookshelf and grandfather clock, and the three bodies left in the cellar. Curiously, the only thing that escaped a fate of ash was a raven figurine."

I couldn't stop thinking about what I had seen on the note, the bold black letters screaming out from the page lying beneath her swinging body: "I could never get rid of the raven!"

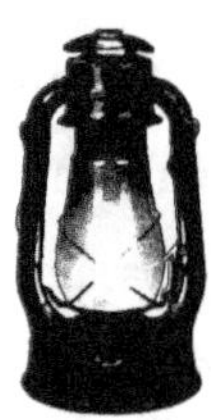

WHERE THE WOODS END

ROBERT SABALA

ROBERT SABALA

With this excellent resolve for the future, Goodman Brown felt himself justified in making more haste on his present evil purpose. He had taken a dreary road, darkened by all the gloomiest trees of the forest, which barely stood aside to let the narrow path creep through, and closed immediately behind. It was all as lonely as could be; and there is this peculiarity in such a solitude, that the traveler knows not who may be concealed by the innumerable trunks and the thick boughs overhead; so that with lonely footsteps he may yet be passing through an unseen multitude. "There may be a devilish Indian behind every tree," said Goodman Brown to himself; and he glanced fearfully behind him as he added,

«What if the devil himself should be at my very elbow?»

49

She hadn't gotten used to the room yet. They had let her sleep in their room for too long and now to get her to sleep in her own bed was going to be a hard transition. It was the third time he'd come to check on her, each time her little saccharine pout waited expectantly for reassurance and comfort. He'd start the investigation with the closet-slowly opened the door in mock suspense and conducted a careful search of the toy chests and the neatly folded clothes.

"No monsters here sweetie" trying his best serious detective face before he closed the doors and continued the search in other suspicious locales around the room. He looked behind the heavy blue and white curtains, and inside the footlocker at the edge of her bed. Each time he would turn back to smile and watch her little eyelids struggle against inevitable. Finally, he'd climb down on all fours and lift the duvet covers that hung over the edge of the bed and stare into the clandestine dark underneath-his smart phone flashlight used industriously to chase the shadows back revealed nothing but the bare wooden floors. Before he was on his feet again she was fast asleep, the little cadence of her breath rose and fell with deep slumber. He stood for a few minutes and watched her sleep- made sure that a spasm of fitfulness wouldn't jar her awake again and begin the nightly ritual anew.

There was something about the room though-he could definitely see it from her perspective. It was almost as large as the master bedroom, but more sparsely furnished to accommodate whatever play she might get up to. It made the whole thing seem a bit lonely at night, and he thought maybe it might do to buy her a dog or a cat to keep her company. He picked up a little as he backed out quietly and took a small pile of books from the floor and returned them to their proper place on the bookshelf next to the window. He stared for a moment at his backyard and let his eyes wander back and forth and looked for nothing in particular. His home sat on the edge of a ticky-tacky subdivision that was never truly completed. Never lived in homes sat unused kept only by the cleaners and landscapers, employed by the bank who owned the properties, trawled the neighborhood bi-monthly. The east side of the house overlooked a half formed ghost town and the west, where his little girl's room sat, faced the overgrown woods that crept up to the edge of their property.

He never liked wilderness, not that the bare woods that grew around them could be called wilderness, walk an hour in those woods and you'd hit a major road, but still he couldn't help hate the idea of her getting lost even for a little while out there. There was a slight breeze that blew in and rustled the curtains, and though he knew it was nothing he still closed the window. He closed the window and stared at the skeletal trees as they twitched and swayed slightly in the wind.

He didn't shut the door behind him as he walked slowly into the well-lit hallway. It was close to 3:15 in the morning but he didn't feel tired. He headed down the stairs and into the living room and took a seat in the center of the couch. He let the television chatter idly in the background while he waited for his body to want rest again, and wished that his mind could slow down enough to let him relax. But his thoughts again drifted out in into the wilderness. He had always hated the woods he admitted, even when he was a kid, camping had always filled him with a sense of vague anxiety. He supposed there isn't really any other kind but vague. He knew that the edges of the map had been filled in, but you couldn't look out over the trees and not suspend your disbelief for a second-there was always something invasive about nature. The woods always seemed to be lurking on the just on the outskirts of everything known-it lived on the very edge of small towns and rural roads and didn't just wait, but with a long silent vigil… seemed to wait with purpose.

He could hear her tossing and turning in bed again, he sighed and smiled as he got up. He'd only gotten about three hours of sleep and he'd need to be up for work again in a few more. He turned the dial on the stove and watched the pure blue flames click in a small burst. He filled his wife's teapot, placed it on the burner, and produced from the pantry sugar and teabags. Years earlier he'd been introduced to the English style of milk in tea, but as he opened the carton the sickly smell of spoiled dairy smashed into his nose like a clenched fist.

A loud thud came from upstairs and he was immediately sure that she'd fallen from her bed again. He turned off the stove and ascended the stairs a slow exhausted trudge. A peek into the room revealed nothing out of the ordinary; she still slept soundly cocooned in her blankets and cartoonishly snored. He walked around the upstairs and checked the other rooms. The house was so asleep-even the groans of protest from the wooden floor under his bare feet seemed groggy. He satisfied himself that everything was in order before he headed downstairs again, and again carefully began to make complete his pot of tea and attempt to start his Saturday hideously early. He dropped the carton of spoiled milk into the garbage and imagined the satisfaction he'd feel while his son took out the trash later while the tendrils of that smell wafted up at him: take that sleeping family.

Again a thud from upstairs, he switched off the burner again, but with less amusement than the last time. He opened the door to her room again to find her sitting up in bed smiling sweetly at him. "What are you doing up pretty girl?" he couldn't help but ask with faux irritation. She shook her head and laughed quietly but didn't try and answer his rhetorical question. She pointed to the closet with the bemused gesture of a game that had no winners but insomnia. He laughed and checked the closet again, but did so with a cavalier melodrama. He flung the curtains aside in assumed a 1920's pugilist stance to battle whatever monster might spring forth. She began to restrain her mirth putting her hands over her mouth as she shook with amusement. She smiled wide and pointed with concern under the bed. He produced his smart phone again and on all fours lifted the duvet covers and used it as a flashlight again to chase away the familiar obscurity.

His daughters face was wet with tears as her eyes implored with an almost hysterical fear as she lay curled up on the floor. His blood froze and after what seemed like an eternity as she whispered:

"Daddy…help…there's someone on my bed"

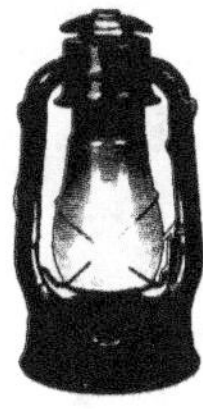

Title: Dark Corner - Short Horror Stories Vol. I

Author: Drew Nicks, Mary Frances Cavallaro
and Robert Sabala

October 2014

darkcornerbooks.com